Rabbit Goes to Night School

Judy Delton
Illustrated by Lynn Munsinger

Albert Whitman & Company, Niles, Illinois

Also by Judy Delton, illustrated by Lynn Munsinger
Bear and Duck on the Run
Duck Goes Fishing
The Elephant in Duck's Garden
A Pet for Duck and Bear

Library of Congress Cataloging in Publication Data

Delton, Judy.
    Rabbit goes to night school.

    Summary: Using his newly acquired magic to do a hat
trick, Rabbit accidentally produces another rabbit
instead of the expected handkerchief and acquires a
new friend.
    [1. Rabbits—Fiction. 2. Magic—Fiction.
3. Friendship—Fiction] I. Munsinger, Lynn, ill.
II. Title
PZ7.D388Rabm   1986   [E]   86-15998
ISBN 0-8075-6725-6

    The text of this book is printed in fourteen-point Baskerville.

Text © 1986 by Judy Delton
Illustrations © 1986 by Lynn Munsinger
Published in 1986 by Albert Whitman & Company, Niles, Illinois
Published simultaneously in Canada
by General Publishing, Limited, Toronto
Printed in U.S.A. All rights reserved.
10 9 8 7 6 5 4 3 2 1

For Kathy with thanks, on our almost-tenth anniversary. J.D.
For Dan. L.M.

I'm bored," said Rabbit to Duck.

Duck was pruning his pine tree. He liked to garden. "You need an interest," said Duck. "A hobby. I think you have too much time on your hands. Perhaps you should come to my garden club next Tuesday."

Rabbit looked at the long rows of beans in
Duck's garden. He looked at the petunias and
the pine tree.

"I don't think so," he said. "I don't like to
garden. The sun gives me a headache, and
the dirt gets under my pawnails."

"Suit yourself," said Duck, going into his shed
for his rose spray.

Rabbit called goodbye. He headed through the woods to Beaver's dam. In front of Beaver's lodge was a sign that said, "Dams for sale here." Beaver was busy building another fine, large dam.

"I'm bored," said Rabbit, standing on the shore to keep his feet dry.

"Maybe you should start a business, Rabbit. With all these orders for dams, I am never bored. Do you like to work with your paws, Rabbit? Do you feel the urge to build things?"

Rabbit shook his head. "No, I don't," he said. "I've never felt that urge."

"Suit yourself," said Beaver, swimming off for more wood.

"Suit myself," muttered Rabbit. "That is just what I would do if I knew how."

On the way home, Rabbit saw a sign outside
Town Hall. "Improve your mind," the sign said.
"Sign up for night school."

Night school sounded more interesting than day school. Rabbit looked over the list of classes. "'Typing, dancing, jazzercise, painting,'" he read. None of these appealed to him. "'Sewing, gardening, magic.' Magic!" he said aloud. "Learn magic to amuse yourself and entertain your friends."

"That's it!" Rabbit cried. "If I learned magic, I would not be bored! Magic would keep me busy."

Rabbit ran into Town Hall and signed up for the magic class. "It begins tomorrow, Rabbit," said the mayor. "You are just in time."

The next evening, Rabbit was the first one to arrive at class. When everyone else was there, the teacher said, "Tonight we will learn how to pull a handkerchief out of a hat."

Rabbit was so excited he jumped up and down in his seat.

"First, we must learn the magic words," said the teacher. She placed a big black hat on the table. She showed the class that it was empty. Then she spread her empty wings over the hat and said,

Abra cadabra ala cazat,
bring me a handkerchief out of this hat!

The teacher pulled a large red handkerchief
out of the hat. She waved it over the heads of
the students.

The audience squealed with delight.

"Now," she said, "I will put the handkerchief back into the hat and make it disappear."

She showed the class the empty hat. Then she placed the red handkerchief in the hat. She spread her wings over the hat and said,

> *Abra cadabra ala cazeer,*
> *make this handkerchief now disappear!*

She tipped the hat toward the students, and they could see that it was empty.

"Amazing!" said the class.

The next time the teacher did the trick, the same thing happened. Only she pulled out a blue handkerchief instead of a red one.

The students practiced saying the magic words. Then the teacher said class was over. "Be sure and practice this trick at home," she said. "Remember, you must say exactly the right words. Practice makes perfect."

Rabbit was very excited about his new interest.
"It suits me! It suits me!" he sang on the way
home.

The next morning he bought a tall black hat.
Then he invited Duck and Beaver to come over
to see his magic trick.

The two friends sat down on Rabbit's couch.
"I'm so glad you found a new interest," said
Duck politely. "It seems to suit you," added
Beaver.

Rabbit showed them the black hat. He turned it
around and around and upside down so that
they could see it was empty.

"There is nothing in this hat," said Rabbit.
Duck and Beaver nodded. "Not a thing," they
said.

Rabbit put his paws over the hat. "Now listen
carefully," he told his friends.
Abra cazabra ala bazat,
bring me a hanky out of this hat!

Duck and Beaver watched closely. Rabbit took his paws away from the hat and reached in to pull out the handkerchief exactly as his teacher had done.

He felt something soft. It felt softer than a handkerchief. And it was *heavier* than a handkerchief. Rabbit had to tug hard.

When he pulled it out, he saw that it *wasn't* a handkerchief. It was a large white rabbit that looked very much like Rabbit himself!

"I thought you said you would pull out a *handkerchief*!" said Duck. "That is not a handkerchief, Rabbit!"

"I must have done something wrong," said Rabbit. "I'll try again. First I must make this rabbit disappear." He put his arms around the rabbit and hoisted him back into the hat. Then Rabbit said the magic words,

Abra catabra ala cabeer,
make this rabbit now disappear!

Rabbit took his paws away from the hat. He tried to tip the hat upside down to show it was empty, but the hat was too heavy to tip. The rabbit was still in it.

"I am not suited to magic, either," said Rabbit
sadly.

"Why, yes you are," said Duck. "You made a
rabbit come out of a hat. That is *certainly*
magic!"

"And you will learn more magic next week,"
said Beaver kindly. "You can ask your teacher
what you did wrong. Then you can make the
rabbit disappear."

Duck and Beaver went home, and Rabbit and
the rabbit from the hat looked at each other.
"What is your name?" said Rabbit politely.

"Rabbit," said the rabbit.

"That is my name," said Rabbit, a bit crossly.
"We can't have the same name, you know. We
will call you Rabbittoo."

"Fine," said the rabbit, who seemed agreeable.

"Have you had lunch?" asked Rabbit. "I was just
about to make my own."

"No, I haven't," said Rabbittoo. "I'd like some
lunch."

Rabbit made them both some carrot muffins.
With the leftover green tops of the carrots,
Rabbittoo showed Rabbit how to make
carrot-top salad for supper. Then he washed
the dishes.

"Do you like to roller-skate?" asked Rabbittoo.

"I don't know," admitted Rabbit. "I have never
skated."

"I will teach you," said Rabbittoo. Rabbittoo
looked in the yellow pages for a place to rent
skates, and he and Rabbit hurried to the shop.
The rest of the day Rabbittoo showed Rabbit
how to skate. By dinner time Rabbit was skating
alone.

"Why, that was good exercise, Rabbittoo!"
Rabbit said. "Let's do it again tomorrow!"

All week the friends skated every morning. In
the afternoons Rabbittoo showed Rabbit how to
carve ships and put them into bottles. And in
the evenings they played Monopoly.

"It is nice to have someone to play Monopoly with," Rabbit told Duck and Beaver one morning. "I am not bored anymore at all. Rabbittoo is good company."

"Magic suits you," said Duck.

"Rabbittoo suits you," said Beaver. "You will miss him when you learn how to make him disappear."

On the evening before the class, Rabbittoo said,
"Do you like to garden, Rabbit?"

"No, I hate to garden, Rabbittoo. Do you like to
build things with your paws?"

"No," said Rabbittoo. "I hate to build things
with my paws."

"We are really suited to each other," said
Rabbit. The thought of losing his friend
brought a tear to his eye.

The next night Rabbit asked the teacher what he had done wrong when he tried to pull a handkerchief from the hat.

"You must have said the wrong words," she said. "You have to say exactly the right words, you know. Otherwise a rabbit might come out of the hat instead of a handkerchief."

"I must have said the wrong words," Rabbit
agreed.

"I will tell you the right words," said the
teacher.

Rabbit thought a minute. Then he put up his paw. "No," he said. "I think I know all the magic I need."

He excused himself and left class early. Then he skipped down the path toward home, where Rabbittoo was setting up the board for a game of Monopoly.